Goldilocks on CCTV

POEMS BY
John Agard

ILLUSTRATED BY
Satoshi Kitamura

F
FRANCES LINCOLN
CHILDREN'S BOOKS

CONTENTS

Puss-in-Trainers

Puss-in-Trainers, that's me.
Puss-in-Boots was great granddaddy.
Fancy footwear runs in the family.
Puss-in-Trainers, the talk of the city.
A feline with a feel for the cool
I gaze at my paws in rivers and pools
A trendsetter, a sleekstepper
with the marmalade moves.
Mine's the whiskers to end all whiskers.
That's why I smile at me from gilt-framed mirrors
And drool on my style in shop windows.
Even bought myself a single red rose.

Me rummaging in bins among fish and veg?
No, I dine with yuppies and celebs
My whiskers are a winner with the ladies
My hip-hot trainers are the bee's knees.
Puss-in-Trainers, eye-popper heart-stopper
Can you conceive of a cat that's cuter?
Sadly neutered.

A GIANT And A Mobile Phone

My name is Blunderbog.
We giants don't go for plain old Bill or Bob.

With my Titan thighs and arms of oak
I can outbrawn any bloke.

My ogre-solid chest will do a barrel proud.
My whisper drowns a crowd.

But sadly my overgrown
fingers are no match for a mobile phone.

Damn this puny handset!
Am I to be outdone by a wimp of a gadget?

My thumb is used to pushing boulders
not titchy fiddly digits.

I guess I Blunderbog
will simply have to bellow my blog

and thunder my text.

There she was on the news,
Miss Goody Two Shoes
caught on CCTV.

Don't look so shocked.
Of course, you know who –
who else but Goldilocks!

Broke into a house
of suburban grizzlies,
a nuclear family

from the sound of it.
Daddy Bear Mummy Bear
and whiz kid Baby Bear.

There she was, tucking in
to a bowl of their muesli.
Every move on CCTV.

How she vandalised a chair
in the nursery
then tried out their jacuzzi

not to mention the towels
marked His and Hers.
And everywhere a trail

of golden curls mixed with fur.
A forensic goldmine.
It appears the police found her

in perfect slumber
at the scene of the crime –
which wasn't very clever.

But the Bears decided to drop
charges for the sake of
happy-ever-after.

And so fairy-tale justice
was seen to be vindicated
and Goldie's parents were sedated.

THE BAD HAIRDAY FAIRY

Who dares make chaff
of the wheat of your hair
and unperm your perm
with invisible fingers?

Who comes unnoticed
to uncurl your curls
to unbraid your braids
with dishevelly flair?

Who drives you in despair
back to the hairdresser's chair
for no rhyme or reason?
Not the wind. Not pollution.

It's only you-know-who,
the bad hairday fairy –
that un-doer of hairdos
who splits ends in split seconds.

PUMPKIN BIKER CINDERELLA

Don't mean to be a pain, Fairy Godmother.
But if it isn't too much bother,
instead of turning a pumpkin to a coach
I'll tell you what - a motorbike would be grand.
No disrespect of course to your magic wand.

I'll eat up the highway with a roar and a rev
on what was once a common veg.
Think what that would do for my street cred.
I'm sure you can manage some mega horsepower.
After all you are my fairy godmother.

I can just see those faces at the ball
when I make my entrance, crash helmet and all.
They'll wonder who's that charming hellraiser
dressed to the nines in daredevil leather.
They'll never guess it's me, ash-girl Cinderella.

Don't trouble yourself with silver slippers.
No, I'll be happy with my biker's boots.
And by the stroke of the midnight hour
I promise I'll be back - and that's the truth -
with some stranded heart for my pinion rider.

Why are you smiling, Fairy Godmother?

A Mother's Advice on the Subject of

Daughters, use your wits.
No denying the feet
those tiny silver slippers fit,
will be walking down the aisle.
And your feet, dear daughters,
will stick out a mile.
So if it's dainty feet
that will pass the slippers' test
and win either of you
a millionaire's *I Do*,
may I suggest
you sacrifice a toe.

Putting Big Feet into Tiny Slippers

You'll be limousine-driven
wherever you go.
Yes, when you're Mrs Prince
one piggy less won't be missed.
Besides, you can always hobble
to the tune of nuptial bliss.
As for those heels of yours,
slice off a bit if you insist.
When those wedding bells ring,
at least your limping heels
will be laughing to the bank.

Daughters, use your wits.
Your big feet are nature's gifts.
So would you rather be
a millionaire's hobbling bride,
or rejoice in your plus-size stride?
Daughters, down life's road,
may your heart, like your feet, be wide.

Did You Say Two Ugly Sisters?

Drop-dead-gorgeous don't apply to us
Do we look bothered? Do we look fussed?

We won't be face-down in no make-up kit
We give the thumbs-up to hair in the armpit

Fluttering eyelashes just ain't our style
Our Barbie dolls made it to the rubbish pile

Our smiles are never rehearsed
We don't keep our hearts in a sequin purse

No, we give fake the cold shoulder
Beauty, we say, is in the ear of the beholder

Never mind the eye, we enchant the ear
From our ugly mouths come song, come prayer.

WAND OR WORD?

The fairy godmother
gets all the credit.
But it's the magic
Word that does it.
Turns the isn't to is.

Oh, the wand's a gimmick
Adds a touch of glitz
Makes the box-office tick.
Audiences don't pay just
to see some frog get kissed.

Like I said, it's the magic
Word that does the trick.
But must have the razzzmatazzz
even when riches turn to rags.
Son, it's called Show-Bizzz.

The Golden Goose Talent Show

1. Laying golden eggs is a thing of the past.
Well, clever but kind of déjà vu.
Listen, kid, audiences want something new.
Show me the goose that lays golden credit cards,
and I'd say, there's talent, the bird's a star.

2. Here's my advice
to an ill-fated goose
with such a rectum.
Listen chum, insure um.

3. But have you heard the one about the poor man
who swopped his goose that laid the golden eggs?
Oh it wasn't a tough decision.
He preferred a hen that laid organic ones.

23

Rapunzel, Let Down

Here he comes, my sweet intrepid mountaineer
who'll dare to scale the summits of my hair.
Would he feel let down or not give a fig
if I confessed to letting down a wig?

But what can there be sweeter and sadder
than a suitor of a girl locked in a tower –
and he gazing up with a bunch of flowers?
Gazing up with one thought in mind. Ladder.

A Tattoo By Royal Command

The teenage princess insists
she wants her navel pierced.
The king and queen
can no longer resist.

They've had enough
of her drama-queen huffs,
her up-in-arms manner,
her slam-door demeanour.

They agree to summon
the Royal Piercer.
Soon her navel's done –
a twinkling bellybutton.

The king and queen thought
it looked rather sweet.
They decided there and then
to give themselves a treat.

'Why don't we have a tattoo
in places considered taboo?'
And so they sent forthwith
for the Royal Tattooist

to inscribe the coat-of-arms
on their unmentionable bits.

Lovesick Frog Prince

Farewell, farewell my crown.
In the waters of a well
now I will sit me down
doing what frogs do best.

Ah, how my heart burns
for that divine-winsome girl
whose necklace I did return
from a well's dark depths.

Will she allow me to share
that pudding from her plate?
Or will she think one like me
a coldblooded vertebrate?

It seems the birds and the bees
get most of Cupid's fame
but sweet to the ear of a frog
is the call of the mating game.

And if this frog should request
a place on her pillow,
will she grant some small token
or reward me with a blow?

So what if the spell
were never to be broken?
I'd squat at the well of her dreams
and consider bandylegs blessed.

No more a tongue-tied prince
with royal duties to endure,
but her croaking troubadour
willing the heavens to rain.

Damsel in Distress Rap

Bring on your shining armour, dude.
I'll be your damsel in distress with attitude.

I'll turn your hunk to butter
    in a flutter of mascara
    flood you in promises
    of happy-ever-after.
I'll lay my head on your chest
    as I put you to the test.
    Spoonfeed your ego's ear
    with sweet nothingness
    and whisper you're the best
    Cause it looks like you're the type
who believe in the hype
Of the damsel in distress.

If I give you my number
will you kiss me out of slumber?
If I shed a tear or two
will you speed it to my rescue?

So bring on your shining armour, dude.
I'm your damsel in distress with attitude.

ACCORDING TO APPLE

I seduced Adam's tongue and his partner's, Eve's.
You could say I caught two birds with one pip.
To find immortal me, you'll have to make a trip
To the golden heart of Hesperides.

One of me a day keeps the doctor away.
Or so they say. And who are you to disbelieve
That once I comatised that Snow-White girl
Until a glass coffin was all her world?

But I'm not always rotten to the core.
I am love's ripeness knocking at your door.

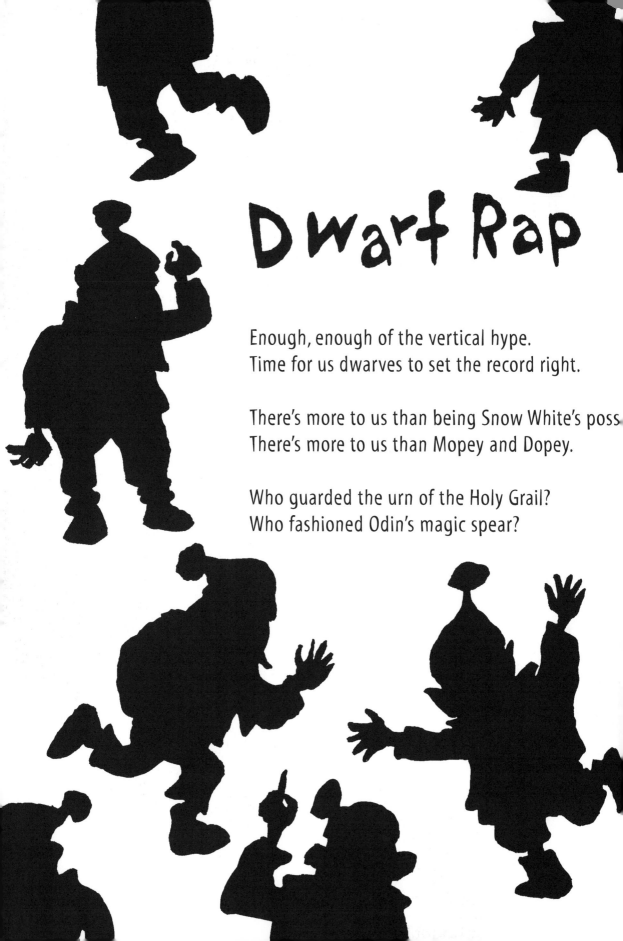

Dwarf Rap

Enough, enough of the vertical hype.
Time for us dwarves to set the record right.

There's more to us than being Snow White's poss
There's more to us than Mopey and Dopey.

Who guarded the urn of the Holy Grail?
Who fashioned Odin's magic spear?

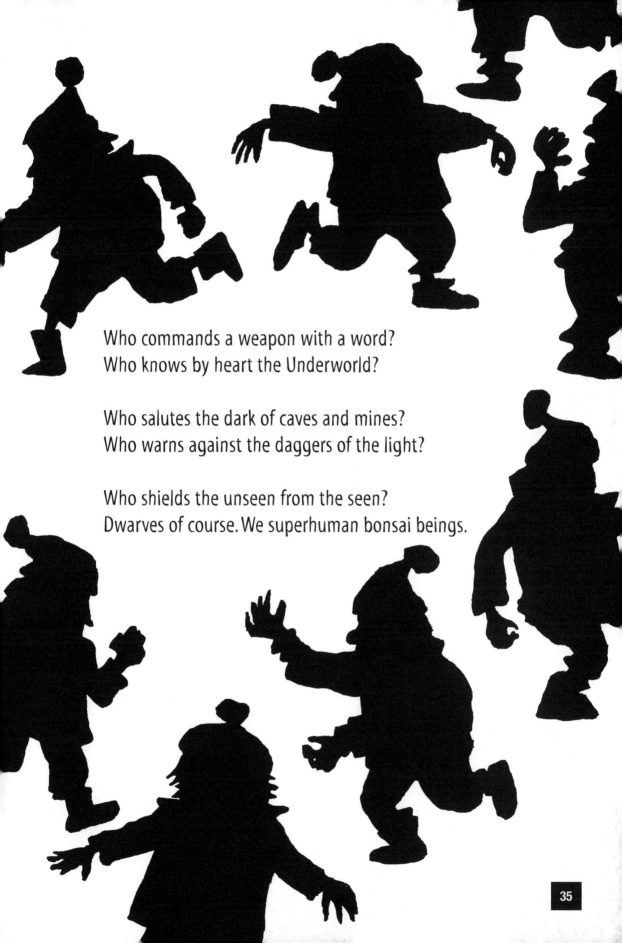

Who commands a weapon with a word?
Who knows by heart the Underworld?

Who salutes the dark of caves and mines?
Who warns against the daggers of the light?

Who shields the unseen from the seen?
Dwarves of course. We superhuman bonsai beings.

STEPMOTHER

Besides, you're not our real mother.

That remark held the chill of ice
and the taste of a maggot.
As if I hadn't tried to be nice!
Where are the gestures they forgot?
Tucking them in at night.
Topping their sandwiches with Marmite.
Joining in their crazy games.
But how can I compete
with a ghost in a picture frame?
Her absence rules my hours.
I must follow in her name.

But stepmums too have vases.
And vases have need of flowers.

REPORTED MISSING

It's no good being streetwise
when you're lost in enchanted woods.
You've tried sticking out your thumbs
but there's no ride to be hitched.
And that nice old lady giving directions
might turn out to be a witch.
You've been reading too many fairy tales.

So you know how the birds gobbled up a trail
of the proverbial breadcrumbs.
And why should you think of a pocketful of stones?
And there's no credit on your mobile phone.
Your only thought was flying the nest called home.
Wonder what your dad and stepmum would say?
And now you reach for scones from an old lady's tray.
And doing the best to mind your language.

Back of beyond but kind of posh. That cottage.
Suddenly, the old dear switches the channel
as the telly flashes your two missing faces.
What if the police should ring the doorbell
or the tracker dogs sniff out your traces?
Then with the look of an old wise crone,
she says:'O you poor dears, here's my mobile phone.
Shouldn't you be texting your stepmum?
The bus doesn't get here for another week.'

The Cloning of Red Riding Hoodie

They did it to a sheep named Dolly.
Why not to a teenage hoodie
with a name like Red Riding Hoodie?
Her code-name shall be RRH 3.

All it takes is one tiny cell
and Red Riding Hoodie will become two.
Not even her grandmother would tell
the original RRH from the new.

The girl will be in good hands –
a scientist of global renown.
You'll recognise Professor Wolf
by his grin and his long white gown.

Seeing two sudden grand-daughters
of course gave Granny a seizure.
Torn between the two look-alikes
she closed her eyes on the future.

Now two identical RRH3s
find themselves lost in fairy-tale woods.
And lost for choice is Professor Wolf,
still with his grin and his long white gown.

His cloning work has proved a success.
But now he faces his greatest test.
One of those two Red Riding Hoodies
will give his Wolf heart reason to bleed.

The big question is: Which one? Which one?

They did it to a sheep named Dolly.
Why not to a teenage hoodie
with a name like Red Riding Hoodie?
Her code-name shall be RRH 3.

All it takes is one tiny cell
and Red Riding Hoodie will become two.
Not even her grandmother would tell
the original RRH from the new.

The girl will be in good hands –
a scientist of global renown.
You'll recognise Professor Wolf
by his grin and his long white gown.

Seeing two sudden grand-daughters
of course gave Granny a seizure.
Torn between the two look-alikes
she closed her eyes on the future.

Now two identical RRH3s
find themselves lost in fairy-tale woods.
And lost for choice is Professor Wolf,
still with his grin and his long white gown.

His cloning work has proved a success.
But now he faces his greatest test.
One of those two Red Riding Hoodies
will give his Wolf heart reason to bleed.

The big question is: Which one? Which one?

WOLF

Touch my legendary pelt
and be lost in wonder.
Why would I want to put on
sheep's clothing?
I am no false prophet.
I need no disguise.
I can have your skin
in a twinkling of teeth.
But you would have me
the butt of a joke
to a family of pigs –
grist for the mill of your fables,
my guts an easy trophy
for some woodcutter's axe.
Forever the big bad loner,
I who suckle the stars
and lullaby the moon
now roam the mansion of your fear.
But don't I look good
in your grandmother's nightdress?

Iron Jack

Iron Jack considers himself
a member of the manly pack

He's been to the wilderness
to the Gulf war and back

But the sight of tenderness
is too much for Iron Jack

Pass a hankie to Iron Jack
his cheeks are starting to crack

There's a sniffle in his throat
and a lump in his six-pack

No, it isn't an easy ride -
this inner horse

called your feminine side.

Road Of Granted Wishes

'Excuse me, wise one,' said the simpleton.
'Is this the road of granted wishes?
Does it lead from rags to riches?
And do I really have to scratch
a wart-studded back where it itches?'

'Too right, young man,' replied the old bag-lady.
'Therein lies the fine print – the catch.
Try your luck on a back such as mine.
Trust me, there's jewels in me warts.
One little scratch brings out their shine.'

Then he who was most simple of heart
asked: 'And what will a little kiss bring?'
'That's for my back to keep under wraps
and for your kindly lips to unwrap,'
said the old one with eyes still twinkling.

'As you wish,' said the simpleton,
'for I've been taught to respect my elders.'
And so one thing led to another -
a back-scratch to a spell-breaking kiss
that transformed her to the girl next door.

To think his riches were under his nose.
To think just over a fence lay his bliss.

Frog on the Mantelpiece

Grandpa sits near the fire
lost in December's glowing log.
He nods towards the mantelpiece
and a picture of a frog.

'That's what I looked like,
before your Grandma came along
and changed my life with a snog.
Now the old dear's gone
it's back to being a frog.
This old armchair
will do nicely for a bog.'

And now we could swear
in a room where the clock has stopped
a small croak times the air.

A WOODCUTTER'S SON

Ain't mine the hand that felled the tree
that gave the wood that made the seat

for your aristocratic arse?
Yes I'm a woodcutter's son.

So tell me the old familiar one
about a woodcutter's son –

how I've got a chip on my shoulder
how I've got an axe to grind.

Go on, tell me another one
as if I haven't heard it all –

how I'm thick as two planks
how I can't tell the wood from the trees.

Have you finished talking down
to us common folk?

Well you can talk from your high horse
till your blue blood runs dry

Remember you're not yet out of the woods
Remember you're not yet out of the woods.

Beast:

I have no desire
to return
to princely attire.
I'd rather ponder
my ghoulish
reflection.
Spare me,
dear girl,
your spell-
breaking kiss.
Let me stay one
with fangs and fur.
Let me suffer
your beauty
while I preserve
this beastly bliss.

A BEAST AND A BEAUTY

Beauty:

Very well,
dear beast.
As you wish.
I'll not break
the spell
with a kiss.
Since you prefer
to be fanged
and furred
and my beauty
only disturbs
your reflection,
I'll leave you
to ponder
your beastly bliss
and find some other
beast to kiss.

WHAT'S IN A NAME?

My name my name
my name dearer to me
than winning the lottery
my name the core of me
the very soul of me
my name the key
to the door of me
my name the sound
that trills
to the note of me
my name the vessel
that fills
to the spill of me
for I am Rumpelstiltskin
known by that name
only by my dwarf-born kin.

Ah Rumpelstiltskin
no more a secret
hushed for all ages
but now big and bold
across tabloid pages.
Damn whoever told
my name my name
to the paparazzi
for they have spilt
the beans of me
unlit
the spark of me
unsung
the lark of me
unstrung
the bow of me
tolled
the very bell of me
indeed tweaked
the inner nose of me.
Whoever it was that sold
my story to the press.

May they be bone-weak
May they be hell-blessed.

Hag Chant

We rolls the dice. We deals the cards.
And in our gob we sticks a fag.
Our hair's a rag, our cheeks are crags.
We toothless ones whose tit-bits sag.
Who cares if your kind call us hags.
Our kind won't grace your glossy mags.
Our mouths you scheme to gag.
Ours the tongue that wisdom wags.
Ancient tales we tittle-tattle.
Prophecies we prittle-prattle.
Incantations we caw and cackle.
Long dumb voices we dare unshackle.
We keepers of the dream, hail the hag.
We feeders of the flame, hail the hag.
We who count the ones in the bodybag.
We who name the dead under your flag.

NOT MY UNCLE BLUEBEARD

It was all over the newspapers.
I thought there must be some mistake.
No, not him, not my uncle Bluebeard –
anything but a serial killer.
But there it was in black and white.
The shock of bodies in the basement,
the very basement where I played
and where the ghost of my innocence
still rummages among dark cupboards
for crystal jars filled with goodies
that twinkled like stars in a sky of glass.

I could still see him dying his beard
that mysterious blue that made the neighbours
think him vain or weird, to say the least.
I should be part of the crowd outside
shouting 'Bastard' and 'Evil beast'
but I'm still that girl on my uncle's knee
feeling as if I had possessed the key
to childhood's carefree doors
when blue meant sunny skies and cornflowers,
not the profiled chin of a serial killer.
No, not him, not my Uncle Bluebeard.

I'm still learning how the heart's chamber
keeps its demons unfathomable.

Mirror Mirror

I am the mirror on the wall.
Dare to look into my telling glass.
I speak the truth to all who ask.

Like my distant cousins, Moon and Sun,
I too delight in revelation.
I will show your future to your past.

Wipe from me the dust of your deeds. Try.
I reflect the you behind the mask.
And my one fault is I cannot lie.

So come on. Ask the burning question.
Break me, if my answer displeases.
I speak louder when I speak in pieces.

SLEEPING BEAUTY AWAKES

Sleep spread through the palace like a virus.
Even the horses and corgis nodded off.
Will Sleeping Beauty never return to us?

Experts monitored her every twitch and snore.
When she woke up a hundred years later
the paparazzi were outside her door.

She made headlines: The Girl Who Slept A Century.
And then she became an overnight success
when Sotheby's auctioned her nightdress.

Yet a hundred years is a long time to snooze.
How could she catch up with all the world news –
all the sleepless reality she'd missed?

And she would think of that spell-breaking kiss –
how princely lips like the softest of scissors
had come to snip the threads of her slumber

and return her to a place called the future.

JOHN AGARD is one of the most popular and highly-regarded poets writing in Britain today. In 2013 he was awarded the Queen's Gold Medal for Poetry for *Goldilocks on CCTV*. His poetry is on the GCSE syllabus and he performs at Poetry Live events throughout the UK. His book for teens, *The Young Inferno*, won the CLPE Poetry Award 2009, was nominated for both the Carnegie and Kate Greenaway Awards in 2010, and was shortlisted for the 2010 UKLA Award. John lives in Lewes, Sussex, with his partner, the poet Grace Nichols.

SATOSHI KITAMURA was born in Tokyo, but moved to London in the 1980s, since when he has written and illustrated twenty of his own books and illustrated many more, including the classic picture book *Angry Arthur*, with Hiawyn Oram, and *The Young Inferno* with John Agard. He has won many prizes for his illustration, including the Mother Goose Award, the National Art Library Award, the New York Times Notable Book of the Year Award and the Smarties Prize (Silver).

THE YOUNG INFERNO

ISBN: 978-1-84780-109-8

"A total triumph" – *School Librarian*